painting him mine

ARIELLA ZOELLE

Dedication

For the skeptics who think doodling on money is a felony.
Relax, it's just love laundering.

Author's Note

Fun fact: This book started life as *Painted Hearts*, a serialized story on Amazon's now-defunct Kindle Vella platform. RIP Kindle Vella—you were strange, and no one ever really knew what to make of you.

Because readers had to unlock chapters with tokens, I kept them super short so finishing the story wouldn't cost a fortune. That's why the chapters and pace here are breezier than my usual books.

As for Ezra, he was originally named Liam, but once I realized "Liam" spells "mail" backward, I couldn't unsee it. My brain short-circuited, and Liam became Ezra faster than you can say first-class postage. No shade to anyone named Liam—it's a great name. Don't mind my weirdness.

This novella is meant to be a quick, fun read that's all about the flirty, steamy vibes. I wasn't aiming for a deep-dive into a realistic romance, so if you're after a book with more depth to the story, check out my full-length novels or my Zarina Aston books if you want a true doorstop book.

But if you're in the mood for a quick read about two guys ready to fuck from "Hello" and experience insta-love on high-speed, then this is about to be your new favorite book!

Chapter One

MAURICIO

"HERE'S YOUR CHANGE. Have a nice day," the barista said with a bright smile.

I accepted it with a word of thanks before heading over to wait for my coffee by the pickup area.

Diego laughed as I pulled out my wallet. "I can't believe you still pay for stuff with cash. It's so much easier to tap your phone on the reader."

"This feels like I'm spending real money and not just moving fake numbers around in the ether." I had a thing about having all my bills face-up, so I flipped my backward ten-dollar bill. To my surprise, there was something unexpected on the front.

Someone had transformed the portrait of Alexander Hamilton into Vincent van Gogh. In the empty space around him, there was a spectacular color pencil sketch of *Starry Night* in the background that was exquisite enough to make my jaw drop. The blue, purple, and yellow swirls of the evening sky were quite striking. As a fellow artist, their talent amazed me. Down in the bottom margin, there was a tiny message in neat handwriting:

LOVE WHAT YOU SEE?
555-652-8745

Diego made a surprised noise when he saw what I was holding. "Whoa, they gave you fake money?"

Having worked in retail during college, I could tell the feel was all wrong for a counterfeit. "No, it's real, but someone defaced it in the most artistic way possible. How incredible is that?" I was in complete awe of the impressive artwork. Who would do such a thing?

"Isn't that illegal?" He laughed before picking up his drink from the collection counter with a word of thanks to the staff.

"Yeah, but who cares when it's this good?" The longer I looked at it, the more I noticed the little details. It impressed me that the cypress tree wasn't one shade of black but made of dark blues and greens like the original painting.

He sipped his coffee as he continued studying it. "How did they get away with someone accepting that? If someone tried to pay me with that, I wouldn't have accepted it."

I turned the bill over to show him that the back was untouched by the artist's skill. "If they handed it over this way, she probably didn't notice before she slid it into the register."

Another barista calling out my order interrupted us. I put the ten into my wallet and pocketed it so I could grab my coffee and two vanilla cake pops. As soon as we sat down at a table by the window, I pulled the bill out again to continue inspecting the artwork. "Seriously, this is incredible." I held the money up for him to look at again. "Why are you not blown away by this?"

"For the same reason that good sound editing doesn't rock your socks off when it gives me life. Art doesn't make my soul sing like it does for you. But I'll admit, it's pretty cool."

I had to swallow down my urge to fuss at him for insulting something so wonderful by calling it "pretty cool." My eyes strayed back to the phone number at the bottom as I took out one of my cake pops to eat. "Do you think it's weird if I tell the artist how impressed I am by their work? They put their contact info on here, so maybe that's what they're hoping for?"

My friend laughed at me. "You can't actually be considering doing that."

"Why not? They wouldn't have written their number if they weren't interested in hearing from whoever received this, right?"

"Okay, so let's say you reach out to tell them you think they're an awesome artist. Then what? You become friends? Start sexting? What are you hoping happens?"

I shrugged as I finished my delicious cake pop. "Anything could happen. That's the fun of it."

"Feel free to do it later. I need your help on my project." Diego pulled out his laptop so we could get to work.

I tried not to sigh in disappointment as I slipped the magnificent ten-dollar bill back into my wallet again. I'd give my friend my attention now, but I would indulge my curiosity once I was alone. Who had created such an astounding piece of art?

Chapter Two

EZRA

I TOOK a step back from my easel to assess my progress on my masterpiece. Painting a view of the Brooklyn Bridge in the style of Vincent van Gogh's *Starry Night* was an ambitious undertaking, but I loved that kind of thing. I was still in the early stages of the work, but it was already coming together beautifully.

My phone alerted with a text, so I set my brush and palette down to check it.

UNKNOWN

You're amazing.

I arched an eyebrow at the unexpected message from an unfamiliar number before responding.

EZRA

I am, but what makes you say that?

UNKNOWN

Your $10 Van Gogh.

Defacing a ten-dollar bill as part of my practice for my painting had been a silly thing to do. However, I loved the idea of letting fate take the wheel to see what happened with it. I had used it to pay for my coffee that morning, hoping that whoever saw it would reach out. Maybe they would be my new best friend. Perhaps they'd be the greatest love of my life. Or they might demand a refund exchange since I ruined their money by doodling on it. Luckily, it seemed like the latter wouldn't happen.

UNKNOWN

It's incredible! I had to know more about the artist who did something so masterful.

Masterful? That word made my ego purr.

EZRA

You've certainly got my attention. What would you like to know?

UNKNOWN

Who you are and why you did it
would be a great place to start.

My name is Ezra van Housteen. I'm
an artist who lives in Brooklyn. That
sketch was practice for my current
work in progress.

I snapped a shot of my canvas and sent it over to them, then watched the three blinking dots flash as they typed out a response.

UNKNOWN

Wow, Starry Brooklyn Night? How
magnificent! Even unfinished, it's
stunning. I'm in awe of your talent,
Ezra.

I was quickly becoming fond of their effusive praise. Relocating to stretch out on my couch, I made myself comfortable for what I hoped would be a fun conversation.

EZRA:

And who do I have the pleasure of
speaking to?

UNKNOWN

My name is Mauricio Damiano. I'm
a floral photography manipulation
artist.

He sent an example of his art, featuring a black-and-white portrait of a young man. His eyes and the top of his head were covered with pink-tinged purple roses against a fuchsia rose background. While simple, it was a striking image.

A quick search showed an impressive portfolio that spoke of a fantastical imagination that drew me to him. His use of color was spectacular. I checked the bio on his website, where I discovered a profile picture of a gorgeous guy. He appeared to be in his early thirties, with dark hair and a kind smile. Instead of a portrait of a serious artist, he had a playful twinkle in his green eyes that invited me to get to know him better.

EZRA

It looks like I'm not the only immensely talented one. Even at a quick glance, your digital gallery is quite impressive, Mauricio. I'm glad my sketch found its way to a fellow artist who appreciates it.

MAURICIO

I more than appreciate it—I admire it. The more I look at your artwork online, the more amazed I am of you and your skills.

His ego stroking was deeply satisfying. It put me in the mood for a different type of gratification, but first, I had to determine if he was interested in that.

Chapter Three

MAURICIO

IT WAS an understatement to say I was enamored with Ezra. Not only was his artwork incredible, but he was also *gorgeous*. With his blond hair, striking blue eyes, chiseled cheekbones, and impish smile, he was the man of my dreams. Seeing a picture of him holding a paintbrush in his elegant fingers got me all stirred up inside. It flooded me with inappropriate thoughts about other long things I wished he'd touch.

I perked up when he replied to my text.

EZRA

It's even more impressive in person.

It seemed like an invitation I was more than willing to accept.

MAURICIO

> I'd love to see it up close and
> personal sometime.

EZRA

I think we can make that happen. If
you're interested in a more hands-
on experience, I'm open to that as
well.

My mind took a deep dive into the gutter as I entertained a brief fantasy about us hooking up. Pulling myself away from such tempting thoughts, I hurried to reply.

MAURICIO

> I'm DEFINITELY interested in seeing
> more of you.

I blanched when I realized I slipped by saying I only wanted to see him, not him *and* his work. As I tried to type a correction, he beat me to it and made my jaw drop.

EZRA

Naked?

My dick perked up at that tempting thought. I couldn't stop myself from getting drawn into his teasing.

MAURICIO

That depends. Is that also part of the "hands-on experience" you mentioned before?

I bit my lower lip as I waited for his response to come through. The blipping trio of dots mocked me as he typed a response.

EZRA

I certainly wouldn't say no to you stroking more than my ego.

I had a special weakness for fun, flirty, and good-looking men. His playfully perverse retort made me shift on my bed as my pants grew tighter.

MAURICIO

I'd do a lot more than just stroke it if given the chance.

EZRA

Oh, yeah? What else would you like to do to me?

Was he inviting me to sext with him? It was a *very* tempting offer, one which I was more than ready to accept.

MAURICIO

I'd start with a kiss to see if you wanted more.

I held my breath as I awaited his reaction. When it took a while for him to respond, I worried maybe I had read things wrong and he wasn't as interested as I thought?

EZRA

Such a gentleman. Would only one kiss satisfy you?

Exhaling a sigh of relief, I grew more turned on as we began a sexy back-and-forth banter.

MAURICIO

I'm greedy, so one would never be enough.

EZRA

Good, because I'm selfish and want more. Are you willing to give it to me?

I'd give you anything you'd like. Hard and fast, soft and slow, whatever turns you on.

By the time I finished typing out my response, my cock was rock-hard. I sure as hell hoped he was aiming for that kind of conversation because I was horny as fuck and ready to tease him until we both came.

EZRA

The thought of you railing me into the mattress is definitely turning me on right now. My dick is hard enough to cut diamonds, thanks to you. Are you prepared to do something about it?

Desperate for some relief, I lifted my hips to lower my blue floral-print pajama pants down to free my erection. I was dying to touch myself, but I typed back to him first.

MAURICIO

Pictures, or it didn't happen.

I had a momentary debate about whether to submit my passive-aggressive request, but my arousal demanded it. Hitting Send, I stroked myself while waiting for his reply.

To my great surprise and satisfaction, he sent me a picture of his hand wrapped around his erection, which was flushed and begging for attention. Zooming in, I noticed the flecks of paint on his skin that told me he had probably been painting when I interrupted him. It lit a fire within me that had me ready to beg for more.

EZRA

Satisfied?

There was only one appropriate answer to that question.

Chapter Four

EZRA

I THANKED ALL my lucky stars that Mauricio had been the one to receive my defaced ten-dollar bill. Not only was he a fellow artist, but he was gorgeous and down to sext with me on a whim. At the rate he was going, it wouldn't be much longer before I was ready to ask him to take things to the next level in person.

His answer made me groan with need as I jerked off.

MAURICIO

Not until I'm sucking your beautiful dick and swallowing your cum. And that's only the beginning of our fun.

EZRA

Damn right it is. Show me how aroused you are.

I slowed down my pace so I wouldn't come to an early finish. Bless Mauricio, he sent back a picture that I saved to an album on my phone to enjoy again later. His cock stood proudly from a nest of trimmed dark hair, making my ass ache from how badly I wanted to feel it moving inside me. Even his forearm was sexy, adorned with the most beautiful flower tattoos I had ever seen. They were in a different array of styles, ranging from photorealistic to abstract. I longed to trace the outline of the delicate petals with my tongue until I came. It was annoying to type a long response with one hand, but I persevered to drive him wild.

EZRA

Your arm is a work of art all by itself, but add in those lovely tattoos and I'm a goner. Thinking about being held in your beautiful, strong arms really does it for me— especially when I imagine them wrapped around me as I ride your thick, long cock.

MAURICIO

I'm imagining grabbing your thighs hard as I thrust into you, making you moan loud enough to piss off my neighbors.

They're going to hate us a lot more because I won't stop until I'm screaming your name as I come. I'm already crying it out so loudly that my neighbors think you're actually here.

Good, because I like it when you get noisy. Tell the entire world how good it feels to get fucked by me.

I keened as I worked my length. It was exquisite torture of the best kind. But I was getting sick of typing one-handed, so I took a chance and called him.

It was hard not to laugh when he answered on the first ring. "You must have read my mind." He chuckled in a smooth baritone that turned my insides to molten lava. "Let me hear you, Ezra."

"Fuck, your voice is so sexy." Since I was shameless and didn't give a shit about the asshole who lived next door, I had no problem getting loud. "Give me more, Mauricio."

His rumbling growl made me whimper as I imagined him gripping my hips. "Can you handle more?"

"Fuck me harder!" My hand picked up speed as

I raced toward my peak. "I need you to paint my insides with your cum."

"I will as soon as you turn my stomach into a Jackson Pollock painting."

The art reference was enough to send me over the edge. I didn't hold back as I climaxed while shouting his name. "Mauricio!" Moaning with satisfaction, I felt completely boneless after my release.

It seemed to do the trick because he moaned my name before his breathing hitched as he came. Both of us were a bit out of breath as we recovered.

I couldn't resist pushing things further by snapping a photo of my splattered cum on my stomach and sending it to him. "Personally, I think I put Pollock to shame. What about you?"

Chapter Five

MAURICIO

I MOVED the phone from my ear and put Ezra on speaker to check the picture he texted me. If I could have come again a second time so quickly, the photograph of his cum-covered stomach would have done it for me. It gratified me to no end that I was responsible for such a beautiful mess. "That's museum-worthy art."

His laughter was so free and lighthearted, endearing him to me even further. "Want to compare canvases?"

I returned the favor by sending him a snapshot of the evidence of how much I had enjoyed our impromptu phone sex. "Something tells me you'll be pleased." I certainly was.

He hummed with pleasure when he received the

proof of how satisfying our session had been for me. "Oh, I'm *more* than pleased. I'm ready to lick that off you and go for round two as soon our bodies can handle it."

Since I was feeling bold after my orgasm, I didn't let my apprehensions hold me back like I normally would have. There was something almost magical about Ezra that freed me from my normal restraints of decency. "Hopefully, our rematch will be in person next time."

"Oh, you can guarantee it will be. If jerking off thinking about you felt this good, getting to be with you for real is going to be *amazing*." He moaned, stirring my desires once more, although my body was still down for the count.

"I'll make sure of it." It was a promise I was more than qualified to follow through on once I had time to recover.

He laughed again. "Can I tell you how I'm *super* glad you received my Van Gogh sketch and not some little old lady? Because this was a better turnout than even my most optimistic fantasies of how my experiment would turn out. It certainly beats the hell out of Granny giving me a lecture for being naughty by doodling on money."

"Unlike Granny, I'm thrilled by how naughty

you are in every regard." I chuckled when he snickered at my comment. "I feel like I hit the lottery. A gay, sexy artist with a playful spirit is almost too good to be true. Not to mention how talented you are is incredibly arousing."

"We definitely owe fate a cupcake for introducing us. Actually, we might need to upgrade to an entire cake since fate was so generous."

His reaction made me chuckle. "I was unaware that cake was fate's preferred currency. What's the exchange rate?"

"There's a flavor hierarchy that must be obeyed, lest you lose fate's favor," he said in mock seriousness before we both laughed. "I offered a vanilla cake pop sacrifice when I handed over my sketched bill, so I'm guessing it's fate's new favorite flavor of the month."

Even though it was a joke, I was still curious. "What about the time before that?"

"I submitted a red velvet cake, hoping I'd score a showing at a gallery. Fate accepted it and blessed me with a sold-out exhibition."

"Did you bake it yourself?"

He snorted like it was a ridiculous question. "Definitely not. If I baked it, fate would never accept it because I'm a disaster in the kitchen. I leave that up to the professionals."

"Well, it seems like I need to start taking lessons on fate's cake code if I want to get ahead in this world." I leaned over to grab a tissue from my nightstand to clean off my stomach when something occurred to me that made me laugh. "Wow, talk about a coincidence. Maybe there's some truth in your theory."

I could almost hear his grin through the phone. "What makes you say that?"

"I ordered two vanilla cake pops with my coffee at the café."

He laughed with delight. "That's perfect! Absolutely perfect. I told you, it's a little-known fact that fate *loves* cake."

"I'll have to remember next time I need help with something in the future."

"Speaking of the future, what do you say to us starting ours together by meeting up tomorrow night?"

In my orgasmic haze, he could have asked me to elope with him, and I probably would have agreed after such a strange and magical evening with him. "I think it sounds like the beginning of a beautiful relationship."

Chapter Six

EZRA

I WAS ALMOST GIDDY with excitement by the time Mauricio knocked on my door the next night for our date. I opened it to reveal a walking wet dream. Somehow, he was even more attractive in person than he was in his photos online. It looked like a model had stepped off the runway and into my apartment. He was stunning in a teal floral-print blazer with a black shirt underneath, paired with white pants. In his hands, he held a large box. I couldn't wait to find out what was inside it.

"Hello, handsome." I stepped back to let him enter my apartment.

"Good evening, gorgeous," he retorted in his smooth baritone that liquified my insides. The hint of a smirk tugging at his full lips made me want to kiss the hell out of him. However, I was trying to show a little restraint so I wouldn't scare him off by coming on too strong. Then again, if the day before had been any indication, maybe coming on hot and heavy was the way to go with him?

Shutting the door behind us, I pointed to what he was holding. "What's in the box?"

He held it up with a grin. "I brought cake."

I had promised myself I wouldn't act with impropriety, but his adorable gesture lit my fire. Since he was significantly taller than me, I tugged on the lapels of his blazer to bring him down for an appreciative kiss. He won major points for allowing me to stay in control as I staked my claim on his lips with passionate need.

Amusement shone in his green eyes when we parted. "It appears that fate isn't the only one who appreciates cake."

"Oh, I *love* cake." *And I love you for bringing one*, I mentally added. "What kind is it?"

He set the box down on my kitchen counter and opened it. I gasped as he revealed a beautiful bouquet of pink, red, blue, and purple roses, along with colorful peonies. "It's a Korean buttercream flower cake."

I tried to wrap my mind around what he said.

"Wait, are you telling me that those flowers are made of *buttercream*? They look real!"

"Yes, and they're delicious."

It was difficult to suppress my urge to touch one of them as a test. The petals were so soft and delicate; it was impossible to believe that they weren't real. "I've never said this before, but it's almost too beautiful to eat. That's not a cake. It's a work of art."

"Thank you."

My jaw dropped as I stared at him, shocked by what his response implied. "Wait, did you make this yourself?"

"I did." He beamed with pride, which he damn well should with the amount of skill it must have taken to create such realistic decorations. "I've always enjoyed baking and making icing roses. When I discovered the impressive artistry of Korean buttercream flowers, I took some classes to learn how to do them myself. We should put it in the fridge for later."

"I'm going to let you do it because I'm too scared I'll drop it." I was a little too klutzy to be comfortable with taking that risk.

He laughed as he shut the lid and carried the box over to my fridge. When he saw inside, he glanced back at me with a single arched eyebrow. The simple gesture drove me wild with lust. "This is like the intersectionality of a starving artist and bachelorhood gone wrong."

I grinned. "Yeah, I know it's bad. But I get so busy with my art I forget about food. Combine that with being lazy and hating cooking, it's pretty much just an ancillary thing I do to survive."

He slid the cake inside and shut the door. "You'd feel differently if you had good food to enjoy." Coming back over to me, he wrapped an arm around my waist to pull me flush against him. "I'd be more than happy to cook for you."

"That sounds great for later." The revelation that he could cook and bake turned me on too much to worry about eating dinner yet. "Right now, I need to suck your dick before I lose my mind."

Chapter Seven

MAURICIO

MY DICK PERKED up at his offer, but the gentleman in me offered a small protest. "As tempting as that is, my cum isn't a worthy substitute for dinner."

He pushed me back against his kitchen counter, then lowered himself to his knees in front of me. The challenging way he gazed up at me was enough to inspire an erection. "True, but it's going to make for one hell of a good appetizer." He undid the button and zipper of my pants, tugging them and my briefs down. It freed my arousal, which stood at attention and silently begged for him to worship it. His cocky grin made it twitch with need. "*Bon appétit.*"

That was all the warning I got before he put on a show of teasing my length with his tongue. He rested the tip on his pillowy, soft lips, then slid it inside his welcoming, wet warmth. I shifted my stance as he began expertly sucking my dick. As he picked up speed and let me glide deeper into his mouth, I laced my fingers through his blond hair with a sigh. My other hand braced against the counter behind me for support.

I couldn't take my eyes off him. He looked like he was experiencing rapturous joy as he sucked me off with great zeal. The combined sensation of his hand jerking me off at the base of my cock was divine. It had been *so* long since I had enjoyed such a skilled blow job. I gladly surrendered myself to his talents.

As he worked up to deep-throating me, I struggled to smother my sounds of enjoyment. A protracted moan escaped from me as he hummed low in his throat while working my length. His enthusiasm sent me soaring as I tried my best not to thrust too deeply into the feeling. His challenging blue gaze was such a huge turn-on, as was the way he wrapped his beautiful lips around my dick while sucking it for everything it was worth.

I had to bite back a curse when he let me slip free. Instead of leaving me hanging, he switched to jerking me off, which was its own form of pleasure. I thrust into his tight grip in search of relief.

His smile was angelic and devilish at the same time. "Do you want to come in my mouth, or would you rather shoot your load on my face?"

The question made me groan, as both options were deeply enticing. "Let me see you swallow me down."

"Gladly." He guided me back into his wet heat to work my length with vigor, like our lives depended on it.

I cried out, unable to restrain myself when he reached back to grope my ass. It got even better when he used his hold to force me deeper into his throat. "Fuck, I won't last much longer." Not when his mouth was offering me sexual nirvana of the highest order.

All it took was for him to moan around me with a look of pure rapture to make me come. "Ezra!"

He swallowed me down, then licked me clean. The way he wiped the excess from the corner of his lips, then sucked it off his thumb, pushed me to my limits.

Tugging up my pants, I tackled him to the

ground to pin him under me. I kissed him hard, loving the taste of my pleasure on his tongue as it dueled against mine. His erection pressed against me, and I had no intention of letting him suffer. Dinner was important, but I wasn't stopping until he shouted my name as he climaxed.

Chapter Eight

IT WAS difficult to control myself when Mauricio undid the button of my pants and tugged them down a little. I growled in frustration over being constrained. "Fuck it, take them all the way off."

I loved how he didn't need to be told twice. He pulled them off, revealing I wasn't wearing underwear. My hard-on stood proudly, demanding attention.

"Do you always go commando, or was tonight special?" He tossed my pants aside before he took a moment to savor the spectacular view I presented him.

"What can I say? I love to live wild and free." Spreading my legs apart, I ran my fingertips over my entrance. I teased him more by tracing over my balls to run up my rigid length. "I'm down for whatever you want to do, so don't hold back."

Repositioning himself, Mauricio guided my legs over his shoulders before he began teasing my sac. He traced the seam with his tongue before he sucked one into his mouth to toy with. I squirmed under the sensation, getting more worked up as he switched to play with the other.

Just when I thought I couldn't take any more, he held my cock steady as he trailed kisses from the base. By the time he reached the tip, I was shaking with need. "I'm going to lose my mind if you don't start sucking my goddamn dick soon."

"Like this?" The hint of suction he used on the underside of my cock made me groan. "Or maybe you'd prefer this?"

Before I could ask what he meant, he went down on me. It was a shock to my system to suddenly be buried inside the wet heat of his mouth as his tongue teased me. He bobbed his head as he worked me, which earned very enthusiastic reactions out of me as I got what I wanted.

My hands sought purchase in his dark hair to help ground myself against the sudden onslaught of intense pleasure. He rumbled when I raked my nails against him, making me thrust into his mouth with a whimper. The man was a master at blow jobs, which guaranteed that I would come to an embarrassingly premature end at the rate we were going.

He continued teasing me by hollowing out his cheeks while he slid along my length, driving me to cry out. I rutted against him with blind lust. Thankfully, he didn't get pissed when I pushed his head to force him to take in more of me; he simply opened wider and let me slide in deep. It was such a fucking turn-on that he didn't get angry about me topping from the bottom. A lot of my former partners had hated that about me, but it really seemed to get Mauricio going.

When his fingers snuck down to tease my hole, my muscles tensed as it shoved me to the brink of my release. It made me babble with need. "Fuck, just a little more, please, Mauricio, fucking *please!*"

The slightest hint of penetration combined with him swallowing around me was enough to trigger my climax. I shouted his name as I emptied into his mouth, gasping as he drank me down. Sliding my legs off his broad shoulders allowed me to guide him up for a hungry kiss. Our mixed releases would have made me come a second time if I could physically manage. I hugged him like a koala, determined to keep him in place as we continued kissing on my kitchen floor. It was officially my new favorite way to start a date. I wasn't about to let him go when he was the best thing that had happened to me in a *very* long time.

Chapter Nine

AFTER WE MADE OURSELVES PRESENTABLE, we headed to the nearby grocery store to shop for dinner. Ezra held the basket as we wandered around together to collect the ingredients I needed to make tequila steak tacos. It was one of my favorite things to make, especially since it was fairly easy to make but really impressed people with the strong flavors. Holding hands as we walked through the aisles was a surprisingly intimate way to spend a first date. Who knew grocery shopping could be so romantic?

We had almost finished when he seemed to read my mind. "Doesn't this kinda make it feel like we're dating for real? Not to weird you out, but I'm seriously loving every second of it."

I picked up a package of skirt steak to inspect it. Finding it satisfactory, I handed it to him to put in the basket. "No, it doesn't weird me out. I'm also amazed at how natural it feels to be together like this. We feel more like an old married couple than two strangers on a first date."

He squeezed my hand with a happy noise and put a slight flounce in his step. "I'm so glad it's not just me who feels that way. I know a grocery store isn't the best place to have this conversation, but I'm *very* open to being your boyfriend instead of a random hookup whenever one of us is horny."

I chuckled at his reaction. "That was almost romantic."

Ezra stopped to look up at me with an earnest expression. "I'm being serious, which is rare. Everything feels right when I'm with you. And I told you yesterday: I'm fucking selfish and want more. I can already tell that once will never be enough with you. I don't just want you for tonight; I want all of your tomorrows, too."

"That was *actually* romantic." His declaration filled me with an unexpected glow. I kissed him in reward, with a sweet, lingering show of affection rather than a demanding claim. It made the warm fuzzies inside me bloom. "I want that, too."

Our next kiss was a little more passionate. "Good, because while I'm impulsive, my instincts are almost never wrong."

We began heading toward checkout since the steak was the last thing we needed to get for dinner. "And your instincts are telling you to be my boyfriend?"

"No, they're telling me to aim higher than that, so I shouldn't settle for anything less than your husband."

My eyebrows arched in surprise as I glanced over at him. "And that doesn't bother you?"

"You're drop-dead gorgeous, an artist, cook, baker, and have a mouth that would put a vacuum cleaner to shame when it comes to sucking my dick. Why *wouldn't* I want to sign up for a lifetime of being with you?" We both laughed before he turned serious. "Not to get all woo-woo on you, but fate obviously brought you to me for a reason. I'm not going to reject that gift by letting the best thing that's ever happened to me walk out of my life."

I used the self-checkout so we didn't have to wait in line for a cashier. "Well, then I guess it's a good thing I feel the same way about you."

"It is," he said before impishly adding, "and I'm not just saying that because I'm excited that I'm finally going to be able to enjoy delicious food on a regular basis."

After bagging my items, I fed the machine my money to pay for them. "For all you know, I could be a terrible cook."

"If you were boasting about how you're the best chef in the whole wide world, maybe I'd have some doubts. But you have the quiet confidence of a man who doesn't need to brag about how good he is. That's sexy as fuck."

I chuckled as we collected the bags so we could head back to his apartment. "I'm starting to think that *everything* is sexy as fuck to you."

"It is with you," he said, making us both laugh. "I'll show you after dinner how sexy I think your cooking is."

That was something I was *very* much looking forward to later.

Chapter Ten

EZRA

"WOW, my kitchen has never smelled this good before." I inhaled deeply as I savored the delectable scents wafting from Mauricio's cooking. "If this tastes half as amazing as it smells, I'm about to have the best meal of my life."

He chuckled as he stirred the sautéed peppers that would go in our tacos. "If you think this is great, wait until you try my Italian food."

I wrapped my arms around his waist and snuggled against his back with a happy hum. "Something tells me I'm *really* going to enjoy being spoiled by you."

"Hopefully, since I have a tendency to be overly indulgent with my partners. I love spoiling people."

His words got my hopes up. "Does that mean

you'll do sweet things like bring me breakfast in bed?"

"Yes, especially if I've worn you out the night before." He glanced at me over his shoulder with a sexy smirk. "I enjoy taking care of people in *every* sense of the word."

I squeezed him tighter with a delighted noise. "How did I get so lucky?"

Turning off the burner, he began plating up our dinner. "I'm wondering the same thing myself. This almost seems too good to be true."

"Well, I'm definitely getting the better end of the deal. I can't cook for shit, sorry."

He chuckled as we carried the food over to my kitchen table. "I'm sure your other talents more than make up for that."

My stomach rumbled from how amazing everything looked and smelled. "I'm glad you feel that way." I was brimming with excitement at getting to taste his tequila steak tacos. My first bite made me moan as the rich flavors exploded on my tongue. Whatever was in his marinade was downright magical. "Holy shit, it's a food orgasm in my mouth!"

He chuckled at my reaction. "I take it you approve?"

My second taste was even better. I made love to

my taco as I ate the whole thing before answering. When I finished, I put on a show of sucking on my fingers. I grinned as he shifted in his seat. "Mm-hmm. That was *delicious*."

His pleased smile was adorable. "I'm glad you liked it."

"I didn't just like it. I *loved* it." It was a challenge to pace myself when it was so yummy; all I wanted to do was stuff my face until I couldn't move. Starting on my second one, I closed my eyes with a happy sigh as I relished the experience of eating something so tasty. "This is so incredible; I can't believe it came out of my kitchen."

I loved the sound of his laughter. "There's nothing wrong with your kitchen that's stopping you from making good food."

"True, but my short attention span and limited patience for that kind of thing makes it tough." I snickered before I enjoyed another taste. It fascinated me, watching how fastidiously Mauricio ate his own taco without making a mess. That also caused me to realize something important. "I love that you made these, and not just because they're the best tacos I've ever had in my life."

"Oh?"

"In case it isn't blindingly obvious, I'm a down-

and-dirty, no-frills kind of guy. Instead of making something that we could eat with utensils, you made messy and satisfying finger food that's fancy without being pretentious."

He grinned at me. "I think that pretty much sums me up: fancy but unpretentious."

I finished my second taco with another murmur of satisfaction. "It makes me so happy. I *hate* hoity-toity assholes. So many foodies and artists are into that bullshit snobbery, and I'm not here for it *at all.*"

"Then it sounds like we're of the same mindset. I can't stand gatekeeping in any form. Everyone should enjoy art, and not only those with obscene amounts of money. And just because some foods are expensive, it doesn't make them any better. I'd much rather have steak tacos any day of the week than caviar and foie gras."

I started my third taco to stop myself from confessing that statements like those were already causing me to fall head over heels in love with Mauricio.

Chapter Eleven

IT WAS IMMENSELY GRATIFYING to see how much Ezra enjoyed my food. He didn't hold back his visceral enjoyment as he practically made love to my taco. As someone who prided himself on his cooking, it was a huge turn-on that he loved my meal. It made it difficult to focus on finishing dinner and not moving on to more amorous fun.

His pout was adorable as he looked at his last remaining taco with a forlorn expression. "I'm not ready for this deliciousness to be over yet."

"There's plenty more where that came from."

He put on a show of enjoying his final bite, which was surprisingly sensual. I shifted in my seat as my lust stirred in response, getting spun up by how much he appreciated my cooking. That reaction became harder to suppress when he moved from his chair to straddle himself over my lap.

I wrapped my arms around his slim waist as he made himself comfortable. Although we were still essentially strangers, it felt right to hold him close. We fit together so perfectly that it didn't scare me how fast things were moving. How could I be worried about that when it felt like we were meant to be?

Ezra leaned forward to give me sweet, teasing kisses that I savored. "Thank you for an incredible dinner, Mauricio. I'm even more excited about your cake now that I've had a taste of what you're capable of making in the kitchen. I bet it's going to be *amazing*!"

"I'm glad you enjoyed it." I let a little bit of my ego come out to play. "And I can guarantee you're going to be blown away by my cake."

He kissed me again, starting soft and slow before he teased me with a hint of tongue. I opened for him, welcoming him as he staked his claim on me. As our kisses grew more heated, he wrapped his arms around my neck as he sensuously rocked his hips against me.

It made me hunger for something much more satisfying with food. While I was eager to give myself over to more pleasure, I still felt I owed him the courtesy of cautioning him. "If you keep it up, you're going to make me want a lot more than kissing."

"Good, then that means you're getting the right idea." He smirked before he tugged off his blue sweater and cast it aside, revealing his beautiful body to me.

My hands slid up from his slender waist, along the curve of his spine, and up to his shoulders. While he had a slim build, he had the toned physique of a swimmer. I wanted to pin him under me and worship every inch of his beauty until he came with my name on his lips. Tilting his head to the side, I began trailing kisses from his shoulder up to his neck. Sucking on his earlobe earned me a breathy sigh of pleasure that made my pants grow even tighter.

Ezra laced his fingers through my hair as he shifted on top of me, allowing me to feel the start of his erection pressing against me. "Ready to do this in bed?"

I didn't need to think twice to answer that question. "Hell yeah."

He scrambled off me and led me over to his unmade bed, which was shoved into the back corner of his tiny studio apartment to make room for his large easel. I could only see the back of his canvas, but it piqued my curiosity about what he was working on. However, as he tugged my shirt off, art was the last thing on my mind for once.

The sight of my tattoos caused Ezra to moan as he ran his hands over the ones on my chest. He followed the path to the flowers that wound around both of my arms. "I can't wait to study your garden of earthly delights later."

One of my eyebrows quirked up. "Did you just make a Hieronymus Bosch joke?"

"Fuck, it's *so* sexy that you picked up on that." He tugged me down for a demanding kiss that had me fumbling to get rid of the rest of our clothes in between bouts. It was a toss-up for who was more turned on by his reference to a Northern Renaissance painting triptych from the late 1490s by an Early Netherlandish master. I had never had anyone talk nerdy to me about art history, but it was officially my new favorite thing.

Once we were both naked, he shoved me onto his bed and got on top of me, clearly determined to kiss the daylights out of me. I wasn't about to stop him from enjoying himself when I was having a great time, too.

Chapter Twelve

EZRA

HAVING Mauricio get my Hieronymus Bosch reference officially tipped me past the point of infatuation, straight into true love. I had always scoffed at people who said they knew after one dinner that they would marry their date. Now, I was ready to elope as soon as we finished fucking.

As I continued kissing him like my life depended upon it, I rubbed my erection against his in search of exquisite friction. I was torn between wanting to explore his tattoos and having him give me the deep-dicking of a lifetime. It became harder to think as his hands wandered all over, teasing any part of me he could reach with a light touch. But if I didn't pace myself, I was going to come to an embarrassingly early finish.

With a monumental effort, I sat up to give us both a moment to catch our breath and take a few beats to help me calm down before I came just from the foreplay. "Do you like Bosch?"

He burst into laughter at my casual question that interrupted our passionate make-out session. "Who doesn't?"

"I can count on one finger the number of people who have been in my bed and known who Bosch was and what he painted." It pushed me to test the limits of his knowledge. "What's your favorite thing in that triptych?"

"My favorite side is Hell, obviously. The pig wearing a nun's habit makes me laugh. Not to kill the sexy vibe, but I'm a big fan of the Prince of Hell bird-man eating humans and shitting them out. Oh, and the scrotum bagpipe on top of the Tree-Man. That painting is wild, especially considering the era it was painted. I feel like every time I look at it, I see something new."

I hadn't been prepared for him to not just get the reference but actually *know* the painting. Instead of wrecking the mood, his answer turned me on even more. It drove me to lean down and start kissing along the trail of flowers from his shoulder, then down his arm. His artwork was lovingly rendered down to the smallest detailed veins in the petals. I looked forward to spending hours studying them and learning the story behind each one. "Why flowers?"

"Because they're ephemeral yet eternal."

His answer left me puzzled, thanks to all the blood rushing south. "Sorry, I'm too turned on to think right now. How is it both?"

"They're ephemeral because flowers only bloom so long before they wilt and decay. There's beauty in how flowers remind us to treasure what we have before it's gone too soon. But at the same time, they'll bloom back to life the next year for an eternity. It's an endless cycle of death and rebirth that fascinates me. I do my best to capture their glory and use that to elevate my art."

I placed a kiss on the blue orchid on his inner wrist. "That's beautiful, Mauricio. I've never thought about flowers in that light before."

"My mother is a florist. When I was a kid, I thought she was a floral grim reaper," he said with a chuckle. "But she celebrates their brief lives by making them as beautiful as possible."

"A floral grim reaper sounds *awesome.*" I kissed the purple-and-pink rose by his elbow as I worked my way back up his arm. "That's really sweet of her. No wonder you're so thoughtful."

"She always says that whether you want to celebrate love or comfort someone in a time of grief, flowers are perfect for every occasion. You send them as a sign of love to your partner, to offer friends and family well-wishes on recovering from an illness or mourning the loss of someone important. Sometimes, you gift them just-because. There's never a wrong time to give flowers because they have a language that speaks without words. As I got older, I realized how right she was."

"No wonder you see the world with such beauty." His answer made me fall for him a little more. I sat back and rubbed my hand over the unmarked skin above his heart. "Maybe someday, you'll let me design a flower right here to show how much I love you."

The words had slipped out of my mouth without permission. In my panic, I considered saying something joking to downplay my slip, but something inside me whispered that I shouldn't take back the words I hadn't meant to say. I held my breath as I waited for Mauricio's reaction. Just to be on the safe side, I said a silent prayer for him to be okay with my accidental confession and that I hadn't just ruined everything. Maybe if I got lucky, he'd feel the same way about me, too.

Chapter Thirteen

IN MY AROUSED STATE, I wasn't sure if Ezra was talking about already loving me or feeling that way about me in the future. Regardless of how he meant it, I would be the luckiest man in the world to be loved by someone as amazing as him. His confident expression gave way to a nervous one, as if he feared he said something he shouldn't. I hurried to reassure him. "I'd be honored to have your artwork there."

Relief washed over him. "I'm the one who would be honored." He bent down to kiss the blank canvas above my heart that I hoped he'd fill in someday. Sitting back, he turned his attention to the other side of my chest. He rubbed his finger over the first flower he encountered. "Wow, a Dutch tulip!"

If I thought him bringing up Bosch's *The Garden of Earthly Delights* was sexy, it was nothing compared to the aphrodisiac of having him recognize one of my art history flowers. "You've got a good eye. That's a Viceroy yellow tulip with red striations from Ambrosius the Elder Bosschaert's *Flowers in a Glass Vase* from 1609."

He gasped when he continued his exploration and found my entwined cluster of Vincent van Gogh's sunflower, iris, and almond blossom. I had expected Ezra to be impressed by them, but his actual reaction caught me off guard. "Marry me."

I couldn't stop myself from laughing incredulously. "What?"

The fear in his eyes was gone. Instead, he looked at me with hopeful determination as he repeated himself. "Marry me."

"Seriously?"

It was clear that he wasn't joking, but I wasn't quite sure how to feel about that. "Very."

"Right now?"

"It doesn't have to be today or tomorrow. But I *need* you to marry me. You're literally my dream come true. It's like fate made us for each other." He traced the outline of my Van Gogh iris. "This is just further proof that you're mine."

When everything about Ezra seemed to be magical, it was tempting to agree to his whim and see where life took us. "You're seriously proposing to me on our first date?"

Ezra took my left hand in his and brought it up to his lips to kiss my ring finger. "I am. There are too many signs pointing to you as being the one to ignore. You're perfect for me in every single way. And I'm everything you need, even though you don't know it yet."

"Are you?"

"I absolutely am." He guided my hand to wrap around his straining erection, moving it in tandem with his to stroke his length. "I'd be happy to prove it to you if you have any doubts."

His claim piqued my curiosity. "Oh, yeah? How would you do that?"

He leaned forward to brace his hands on the bed over my shoulders. "Fuck me and find out." He lowered himself to give me a tantalizing kiss, teasing me with a hint of tongue, making me want more. "Once you come inside me to mark me as yours, you'll have all the answers you need when you see your cum spilling out of me."

His vivid description turned me on even more. I reached up to pull him down as I kissed him hard, moaning against his lips as our tongues battled for dominance. If he wanted to be mine, I wouldn't hesitate to accept what he was offering. It was already apparent I'd never be satisfied with a single evening with him. Although we had known each other for such a short time, I knew with startling certainty that a lifetime of him was what I desired. It didn't make sense, but when he was naked and on top of me, I didn't care about that at all.

I reversed our positions as I pinned him under me on the bed. If he was serious about being mine, then I'd stop at nothing to have all of him. I'd claim every inch of him and leave no doubt in his mind that he belonged to me. Someday, we'd make it official, but for now, it would be enough to physically show him that he was all mine.

Chapter Fourteen

I HAD DONE a lot of stupid shit in my life. Proposing on a first date was a new level of what the fuck, even for me. But everything inside me knew with absolute certainty that Mauricio was the one for me. What was the point of waiting an arbitrary number of months or years to declare my intentions? I wasn't the type to bullshit, so coming out and saying he should be mine was much more my style.

Thankfully, Mauricio hadn't gotten angry or made fun of me for putting my heart on the line by declaring we should make a future together. He flipped me over and started kissing me as if he was determined to claim me as his, which was exactly what I wanted. It was just further evidence that he was the perfect man of my dreams.

Wrapping my arms around his neck, I buried my fingers in his dark hair as he demanded I surrender to him. I opened for him, letting him stake his claim on me with passionate need. His erection rubbing against mine filled me with burning lust. Just when I thought I couldn't take it anymore, he began kissing down my body. And because he was the perfect partner for me, he threw in a few nips along the way to keep it interesting.

Mauricio paused long enough to grab the bottle of lube I kept in my nightstand drawer. He wasted no time in sliding two slicked fingers inside me to start as he continued kissing me all over.

I spread my legs wider apart as my body moved against him, trying to draw him deeper. He drove me wild by toying with my balls while he worked me open. It made me ache with a need for more. I put up with the process for as long as I could before my demanding nature took over. "I'm good, so let's move on to the fun part."

"Are you sure you don't want me to wear a condom?" He withdrew his fingers from inside me, making my heart rate skyrocket.

"I'm absolutely positive. I told you before. I

want you to paint my insides with your cum to mark me as yours."

His eyes fluttered shut at my declaration before he opened them and lubed his cock. He made me laugh when he got up to grab a washcloth to clean his hand with before returning to my side and settling between my legs. I loved how he cupped my ass before he guided his tip into me.

For once, I savored the slow spread as I welcomed him into my body. It was hard not to wax poetic about how we fit together like two perfect puzzle pieces as he pushed in to the hilt. While I was normally a fan of fast and furious fucks, Mauricio started off easy. He rocked against me with steady thrusts as his hand wandered all over my skin to any part he could reach. It had been a long time since I had been with a lover who treated me so gently, which only made me fall for him even more.

I wrapped my legs around his waist to give myself some leverage to move. It felt so good that I didn't speed things up for once. I enjoyed his gentleness in a way I normally lacked the patience for. That served as yet another reminder that Mauricio was the man I had waited my whole life to find.

As he treated me with a tenderness I had never

experienced before, I clung to him as our bodies moved in search of the ultimate pleasure. Moans and sighs slipped from my lips as he made love to me like I was his most beloved treasure. I couldn't get enough of it.

It further endeared him to me and made me want a lifetime of happiness with him. I refused to settle for a one-and-done date with him when being intimate together was the most incredible experience of my entire life. I'd do whatever it took to help him understand we owed it to ourselves to make something work between us. I was confident that my future husband would thank me later for taking the initiative in our relationship.

Chapter Fifteen

MAURICIO

EZRA HAD BEEN RIGHT. As I slid my cock into him, it felt like his body welcomed me home. It was as if my soul had been lost and wandering but finally found peace when I joined with him as one. It was a feeling that no other partner had ever given me before. As my body rocked against his in search of the ultimate pleasure, I had never felt more connected to another person in my life. When I leaned down to kiss him, it felt like a circuit completed between us, bonding him to me.

The rational part of my brain should have panicked that I was falling too hard and fast for it to be a good idea. But I wasn't scared of how intense my feelings were already, despite having known him for barely twenty-four hours. I selfishly wanted more of him, even if that meant doing something outrageous, like accepting his unexpected proposal. Why would I ever say no to a lifetime of feeling so good? The level of ecstasy I experienced while being buried in his tight heat was unmatched by anything else. I wanted all of him, and I wouldn't accept anything less. If he was willing to be mine, I would happily claim him.

His moans and erotic whimpers pushed me to my limits, as did the way his tight channel embraced me. But when he leaned up to place a lingering kiss on my Vincent van Gogh sunflower, it shoved me past the point of no return. I came with a sigh, thrusting until I was spent. Even though he hadn't finished yet, I pulled out of him and rumbled with approval as I watched my cum dribble out of his pink pucker. It made some primitive part of my brain eager with excitement as I reached down to tease his hole, watching more squirt out as I pushed my fingers deep into him.

I shifted positions so I could go down on him while I pumped my fingers in and out of him. He cried out as his body moved blindly in search of release. His hands found purchase in my hair as he squirmed under me. I enjoyed keeping him right on the edge, teasing him until his body tensed in anticipation of his climax, and then backing off. Even when he pushed my head down to force me to take more of him, I continued revving him up and staving off his release a little longer. Getting him worked up was reawakening my lust, and I reached down to encourage my dick back to hardness.

A sob escaped from him. "Please, let me come, I'm begging you!"

I let him fall from my mouth, earning me an angry swear. "You come when I say you do."

He whimpered with frustration as he thrashed under me. "*Please*! I'm *so* close." He growled when I stopped him from touching himself. "Damn it!"

There was something gratifying about having Ezra depend on me for his pleasure. It gave me the boost I needed to be hard enough to slide back into his slick heat. As I pushed into him, he arched off the bed with a shout. "*Yes*!"

Whereas I had been gentle before, this time I gave it to him a little harder since I knew he was desperate and on the brink. I teased him by speeding up and slowing down with a mix of deep and shallow thrusts as we rutted like animals in heat. He raked his nails down my back as his thighs gripped me hard. It was endearing hearing his incoherent, erotic babbles as he raced toward his climax.

He tensed around me, signaling that it wouldn't take much more to send him over the edge. All I had to do was reach between us and jerk his cock twice to trigger his orgasm. He shouted my name as he came in spurts that almost reached his chest.

The sight of him at the apex of ecstasy took me to the edge. Guiding his legs back onto the bed, I pulled out and straddled over top of him. Before I could finish myself, he did it for me. After a few strokes, I came on his stomach as I gasped his name.

Breathing hard from the effort, my body trembled from having two intense releases back-to-back. I reveled in seeing our cum mixed on his skin. It made him look thoroughly debauched as he was strung out on pleasure. But more importantly, it made him look like *mine*. I loved everything about it. Seeing him covered in evidence of our pleasure filled me with absolute certainty about how much I needed him in my life. But was I really going to accept his marriage proposal on our first date?

Chapter Sixteen

EVERY FIBER of my existence thrummed with intense sexual satisfaction. I felt thoroughly used in the best of ways and pleasantly full of Mauricio. I also took great pleasure in mixing our cum together on my skin, even as more of him trickled out of my hole. Unable to resist, I swiped some of the cum off my stomach to put on a show of sucking it off my fingers while looking deep into Mauricio's green eyes.

He stared, transfixed by my deliberate display. It gave me a heady feeling that he couldn't stop himself from watching as I acted like I was giving my fingers a blow job. If either of us was physically capable of it, I was sure we'd go for round three because of my teasing. Even though I was thoroughly spent, I still loved getting us both stirred up by my sensual display.

"*Yes.*"

Withdrawing my fingers from my mouth with a wet *pop* for emphasis, I stretched out underneath him in sensuous repose. I gave him a coy look as I asked in a playful tone, "Yes, what?"

"Yes, I'll marry you."

"Wait, are you serious?" I blinked at him in shock. It was a miracle he hadn't bolted for the door the second I popped the question. But I *really* hadn't expected him to take my whim seriously and give me a real answer. Had he really agreed to my outrageous proposal?

"The courthouse is already closed at this hour, but I will marry you first thing tomorrow morning if that's what you want." He reached out with his clean hand to cup my cheek in his palm. "I don't care if everyone else thinks we've lost our minds. All that matters to me is we can enjoy a lifetime of how incredible it feels to be together."

It was too good to be true. His words overjoyed me that I had lucked into finding a man who was on the same wavelength as me when it came to what our relationship could be. I tugged on him to make him come close enough to seal his promise with a passionate kiss. It slowed to gentleness, flooding my heart with newfound love. We were breathless when we paused.

I smiled up at him with all the affection for him that had already rooted itself deep inside my soul. "You really are the perfect partner for me."

"As you are for me." He shifted to stretch out on his side next to me, one arm slung over my chest as we continued resting until we found the will to clean up. "I'll have to make a hell of a wedding cake as a thank-you to fate for blessing me with a fairy-tale perfect husband."

His words made me perk up despite my exhaustion. "Ooh, that's right! We still have your cake in the fridge for later."

"Yes, after we rest a little longer and get cleaned up," he said with a chuckle.

I put my hand on his arm that was holding me and gave it a squeeze. "Sounds good to me. It's been a long time since I've been so pleasantly worn out."

"Same." He kissed the side of my shoulder, making me giggle. "Not to mention, I don't think I've ever felt this satisfied in my life."

"Same times two." I closed my eyes for a moment with a happy sigh, enjoying the echoing pleasure resounding through my soul. "Maybe later, you can tell me a bedtime story about some of your flower tattoos."

His deep chuckle made me shiver with residual lust. "Something tells me we would get distracted from sleeping if you started exploring my body that way."

"I'd promise I'll behave, but I don't want to lie to you." We both laughed. "In case it isn't obvious, I'm an open book without a filter. I'm incapable of lying because my poker face is nonexistent."

"That's a good thing." He squeezed me tight in a one-armed hug. "Honesty, trust, and communication are some of the most important parts of being in a healthy relationship."

I grinned at his words. "Then I'm definitely the best husband for you. I'm honest to a fault, I'd rather die than break your trust, and I'll never shut up unless I'm sucking your dick."

He rested his forehead against my shoulder as he laughed hard. "You're right. You are absolutely perfect for me in every single possible way. I don't know how I got so lucky."

"Fate must *really* love your cakes in particular." The thought made my stomach rumble, causing both of us to crack up again. "I can't wait to find out why she's your biggest fan once I have the energy to move."

"I promise I'll get you cleaned up and fed as soon as I'm capable of being a person and not a satisfied puddle who is more mush than man."

His choice of phrase made me grin. "I'm *so* going to enjoy being spoiled by you for the rest of my life." The prospect made me downright giddy as I guided him closer for a soft kiss. It was so refreshing that I didn't have to tamp down my reactions so I didn't overwhelm my partner. Mauricio accepted me as I was, and how could I ever ask for anything more than that? Especially when he had brought cake for us to enjoy as soon as we had the energy to move.

Chapter Seventeen

MAURICIO

EZRA INSISTED on taking photos of my cake from every angle before he'd allow me to cut it. My ego purred over his effusive praise for my skills in making Korean buttercream flowers that looked real. He was also extra adorable in his pajama pants with red and pink graffiti grunge ink hearts.

"It feels like you brought me the most beautiful bouquet in the world that's somehow edible." He snapped a few more shots with his phone. "The artist in me thinks it's too pretty to eat and wants to watch you make these incredible flower petals. But my sweet tooth is ready to dig in and see if they're as delicious as they are gorgeous."

"There's only one way to find out." I held the knife over the cake to cut it.

"Okay, one more." He took a final picture before he gestured for me to continue.

"How big of a piece do you want?" I cut into the spongy cake before moving to make a second cut. When he said nothing, I prompted him. "More?"

He nodded enthusiastically. "Yes, please!"

I cut his large slice and laid it out on one of his blue-glazed plates. While I could bake more elaborate cakes, it was a simple three-layer vanilla cake with buttercream frosting. Since he had mentioned eating the vanilla cake pop at the café the day before, it seemed like a safe bet without knowing his other preferences or allergies.

Ezra *oohed* and *aahed* over the layers, taking more pictures of the inside and the slice on his plate. I cut a piece for myself before putting the rest in the fridge for later. We carried our plates over to his kitchen table and made ourselves comfortable.

He wiggled in his chair with excitement, like a little kid at their birthday party. I waited for him to take his first bite to see if he liked it. His reaction didn't disappoint when he closed his eyes to savor the flavor with a moan. "Oh my god, *Mauricio.*"

I was incapable of physical arousal after our previous rounds of fun, but I still responded to the sensual way he moaned my name. It was satisfying to watch him have a semi-religious experience from eating my dessert. "I'm guessing you approve?"

He sucked on his fork after taking another bite with a moan. Clearly, any future cakes I baked for him would have to be enjoyed in private. I would have pounced on him if I wasn't down for the count.

"If you hadn't worn me out earlier, I'd be coming in my pajamas from how incredible this tastes. *Wow*. Do you have any idea how much it's blowing my mind that you created an edible orgasm in dessert form?"

His choice of phrase made me laugh. "I'm glad it meets with your approval."

He cut off one of the pink roses and heaved a contented sigh. "This is officially the best cake I've ever eaten in my entire damn life. You are an absolute master. No wonder fate loves you and your impossibly delicious cakes."

"I'm sure you're exaggerating."

He shook his head. "I may be prone to hyperbole, but I'm one hundred percent serious right now. I'll prove it to you tomorrow."

I waited to respond until I had enjoyed my cake. It pleased me that the sponge had turned out so light and moist. "How are you planning on doing that?"

"You'll see." His impish grin was quite alluring. "I can promise you'll enjoy it."

While I burned with curiosity, I told myself to be patient. "I'm looking forward to whatever you have planned."

Chapter Eighteen

EZRA

MAURICIO'S hard cock pressing against my ass woke me up the next morning. As tempting as it was to take advantage of it, it would ruin my plans. I rolled over, loving seeing his handsome face first thing after waking up. I couldn't wait until every morning started that way.

His green eyes were so beautiful as he gazed at me with sleepy affection. Reaching down, I stroked his erection. "I promise I'll play with this after breakfast, okay?"

"That works for me." He won major bonus points for his amiable reaction. Most guys would have demanded I pleasure them before we started our day. It said so much about Mauricio that he was fine with me not taking care of him right away.

Getting out of bed, I made my way to the kitchen to act out what I had been imagining since the previous evening. I suspected he was going to *love* what I was about to do. If nothing else, it'd more than make up for me not getting him off before getting out of bed.

Mauricio got up to follow me, earning more points with me when he didn't bother putting on clothes and didn't seem bothered by his arousal. "Do you always eat breakfast naked?"

"Nope, but today is special." I pulled the white box out of the fridge with an excited noise.

He quirked an eyebrow at me. "Cake for breakfast?"

"Do you want a slice, or would you prefer cereal?"

"I guess I'll do cake since you claimed today is special."

After dishing out two pieces on plates, we carried them over to my table. Before I sat down, I adjusted my chair to give him an unobstructed view of me as I ate.

He tilted his head as he looked at me with curiosity. "What are you doing?"

"You'll see." With great relish, I took my first bite of cake, moaning as the sweet vanilla taste made my taste buds sing with delight. Somehow, it was even better today than yesterday. It was such a turn-on that Mauricio was an incredible baker and that he had taken the time to make me such a piece of art for dessert.

As I continued eating, I fantasized about him cracking eggs into the flour. My dick perked up as I thought about his powerful forearms as he whipped his cake batter with a whisk. I especially enjoyed dreaming about his large hands doing such delicate piping of the petals. His desire to create something delicious to show me his appreciation was enough to get me going as I sucked another bite off my fork to savor.

At the sight of my erection, Mauricio's eyebrows arched upward in surprise. "Seriously?"

"It's *so* good," I moaned. But I wasn't just talking about the flavor. I loved everything the cake symbolized. His detailed recreations of flowers from buttercream frosting made me adore him even more.

I let my imagination keep running wild. Thinking about him standing behind me, his erection pressing against me as he showed me how to mix the ingredients together, caused precum to bead on the tip of my dick. I loved the idea of him turning me around and brushing some stray flour off my cheek before giving me tender kisses. Dreaming about him patiently teaching me how to make the delicate buttercream flowers made me ache to take myself in hand.

As it always did, my impish nature took control as I fantasized about sucking icing off his finger before I moved down to do the same to his dick as I gave him an appreciative and delicious blow job. In my mind, I drove him wild when I paused long enough to take more icing out of the bowl to coat his length. I then licked the underside clean before putting on a show of sucking off the rest as I went down on him.

Lost in my daydream, I had almost finished my cake. I switched to imagining him fucking me against my kitchen counter as I wrapped my arms and legs around him to hold on for the ride. He drilled me good, laughing when I snuck more icing from the bowl to suck off my finger as he pushed me to my limits. I loved thinking about him speeding up to make both of us come before the oven timer went off.

With my last bite, I imagined him letting me

suck icing off his fingers as he came inside me. It took me over the edge, so I held his gaze as I came with a whimper in real life, without ever having to touch myself. I smirked as I noticed he was rock-hard with appreciation. "Now do you believe me when I say your cake is an edible orgasm?"

Chapter Nineteen

MAURICIO

WHEN EZRA HAD CLAIMED the previous night he would have climaxed from just eating my cake alone, I thought he was joking. But I had just watched him do exactly that without touching himself. No one had ever appreciated my baking in such a sexual way before. To say it checked all my boxes of things that gratified me was an epic under-statement. However, it was hard to settle on a single reaction when I was in utter awe of his erotic performance. "*Wow.*" My dick throbbed from how badly I needed to come, but I didn't dare touch myself for fear of coming to an embarrassingly early end.

He used a napkin to clean off his cum before moving to kneel between my legs. Running his hands up my parted thighs, he stared up at me with lust. He wetted his plush lips before asking, "Will you let me show you how much I appreciate your baking talents?"

I nodded, finding it difficult to form words because I was so spun up from his sexual display. After what he had done, I'd let him do damn near anything he wanted to me.

He reached up to steal one of the icing roses off my unfinished slice of cake, then rubbed it over my erect cock. I held my breath as he started by teasing me with little flicks of his tongue before he worked on sucking me clean. I spread my legs wider as I moved forward in the chair, spellbound as I watched him enjoying my icing like I had never seen before. It drove me wild as he moaned and whimpered around my length as he savored the buttercream.

When there was none left, he repeated the process with a new flower. It was even sexier the second time now that I knew what he intended to do. I grabbed the chair back to restrain myself as my other hand found purchase in his hair. Caressing him as he worked me, I wouldn't last long. Not with the way his tongue drove me wild in its quest to clean every bit of frosting off my arousal.

Switching between deep-throating me and focusing on just the tip, he pushed me to my limits. But an idea came to mind that made me stop him from continuing. I guided him to straddle himself over my lap. As he kissed up my neck to tease one of my ears, I pulled off some cake with icing and held it up to Ezra in offering.

He opened for me, letting me slide it into his mouth. After he chewed and swallowed the piece, he slid my fingers into his wet warmth. His tongue lapped the frosting off before he sucked on them like he was giving me another blow job. Holding my gaze, he moaned around them at the same time he reached down to stroke my erection.

The combined stimulation caused me to explode all over his fist with a gasp. I watched in awe as he let my fingers slip free. He then put on a show of licking his hand clean of my cum with long swipes of his tongue.

"You're definitely my favorite frosting." He sucked his fingers into his mouth to finish cleaning them as he gave me a coy look.

I cupped the back of his neck and pulled him

close enough to allow me to kiss him with a hunger borne from his erotic show. If I had any doubts before about being too impulsive about agreeing to marry Ezra after knowing him for one day, his actions eradicated my lingering qualms. I'd be a fool to let him go when he had proven over and over again that he was the perfect partner for me. I needed more mornings to start the same way. It also excited me to think about giving him sexy baking lessons, although the odds we would burn our desserts as we got distracted were pretty high. It would be a worthy sacrifice to the baking gods to enjoy the pleasures of his body.

Now that we had satiated our lust, it was time to indulge my curiosity.

Chapter Twenty

EZRA

AFTER WE CLEANED up from our breakfast fun and put on clothes, Mauricio wandered over to my easel with my latest work in progress. He stood in front of my canvas to admire it with a look of awe on his face that further endeared him to me. "Wow, this is even better in person. You can really appreciate the impasto detailing in your paint." He glanced over at me. "What inspired you to do this?"

"As a lifelong Vincent van Gogh fan, I couldn't resist the challenge of painting the Brooklyn Bridge at night in his *Starry Night* style. I'm pleased with how it's turned out so far, but I still have quite a way to go before it's finished."

"It's truly remarkable." His smile was beautiful and lit me up inside. "I'm in awe of your talent. As amazing as your *Starry Night* sketch on my ten-dollar bill is, this is next-level awesomeness."

I hugged him to indulge in a cuddle. "I'm glad it brought us together."

He wrapped his arm around my shoulder as he held me close. "So am I. It makes me even more excited to have you design a flower for me."

I slid my hand up to rest over his heart, where my flower would eventually take root on his skin. "I already know what I'm going to do, too."

He covered my hand with his and squeezed it as he pressed it against his chest. "Are you going to tell me, or is it going to be a surprise?"

"I think it'll be more fun as a surprise."

"That makes sense, considering everything about you has been a fun surprise." He leaned down to give me a sweet kiss. It melted me into a puddle as I held on to him for support. "I look forward to finding out what you have planned for me."

"The only hint I'll give you is that it will be a flower like nobody has ever seen before."

He smiled at me with a fondness that made me heady. "I love that it'll be as unique as you."

"It definitely will be." I placed a kiss above his heart. "I'll make sure it's as perfect as you."

"You're adorable." He kissed my forehead with a gentleness that melted me.

Taking his hand, I led him over to sit on the couch. I hesitated before I figured I had nothing to lose by asking. Why start being timid now? "So, while I work on designing the perfect flower for you, how do you feel about engagement rings?"

He stroked his chin as he mused on the subject. "I don't have a specific preference."

"If we tell people we got engaged on the first date, we're going to get a *lot* of shit for it from our friends and family if yours are anything like mine. But what if we wear secret rings just for us?" I got more excited about the idea as I continued. "It'll allow us to celebrate being engaged while letting our friends and families warm up to the idea of us dating without jumping down our throats about moving too fast."

"I like that idea, but I don't think it'll be very secret if we're both wearing the same rings."

His protest didn't deter me. "We can always say the coincidence was one of the things that brought us together. After all, it'll technically be true. I think my friend Etienne can help us."

"How?"

"I promise you'll love it. I just need to check one

thing first." I gave him a quick kiss before getting up to get my phone off the charger on my nightstand. Returning to the couch, I sat next to Mauricio as I texted with Etienne. After a few back-and-forth exchanges, I lit up with excitement. "He said he has them!"

He seemed a bit lost. "Has what?"

Putting my phone down, I moved to straddle myself over his lap. I wrapped my arms around his neck as I made myself right at home. "Etienne specializes in enamel jewelry and art history. He has the perfect rings for us."

"Do I get to find out ahead of time what they are?"

"No, that'll ruin the surprise." I gave him an enigmatic smile. "But we can go there today to pick them up."

"Can I at least get a hint first?"

I tapped my chin as I pretended to think of one. "They'll be perfect for us. Trust me, Etienne's an amazing artist in his own right, so they're going to be spectacular and worthy of our love for sure."

"If you think they're perfect, I'm sure they'll be amazing." His trust in me made my heart soar.

How in the world did I get to be so lucky?

Chapter Twenty-One

MAURICIO

I HADN'T BEEN sure what to expect with visiting Ezra's friend's jewelry store, but a super-posh place for the rich and famous hadn't been what I had imagined when he first brought up the idea of getting wedding rings from Etienne. The decor was modern and chic, with everything white and sparkling as rich people with more money than I'd ever earn in my lifetime browsed the cases for the perfect accessory.

Ezra looked up at me with a grin. "You were expecting something a bit more bohemian, weren't you?"

"This is certainly a surprise."

"Despite how it looks, I promise we aren't going to wipe out your bank account for this." He tugged on my hand to lead me over to where a handsome man greeted us with a friendly smile and wave. His dark hair was perfectly styled to go with his expensive three-piece gray suit that was paired with a pink shirt and tie.

"*Bonjour, mon frère.*" The man's French accent was warm as he came out from behind the counters to give Ezra a hug and kiss both of his cheeks. "*Toutes mes félicitations!*"

Ezra beamed at him with radiating joy. "*Merci beaucoup.*" He gestured to me. "Etienne, this is my fiancé, Mauricio."

He held his hand out to shake, then kissed both of my cheeks. "Congratulations on your engagement. I wish you and Ezra all the happiness in the world."

"Thank you." His words warmed my heart as they made our engagement feel even more real. "It's a pleasure to meet you."

"The pleasure is mine." He returned behind the counters and gestured for us to follow him over to a case. "Come, I have the perfect rings for you both."

Ezra took my hand in his as we followed Etienne, squeezing it as we walked. I loved how his hand felt like it was made for mine to hold.

Etienne pulled out a row of enamel wedding

bands that all had famous post-Impressionism paintings on them. Two Vincent van Gogh ones immediately jumped out at me as they were his *Starry Night* and *Almond Blossoms*. There also were some Claude Monet waterlilies that were equally stunning. "I believe these are what you had in mind, Ezra?"

"Yes, they're perfect!" He picked up the *Almond Blossom* ring and held it out to me. "What do you think?"

Accepting the ring, I studied it closely. The printing of the artwork on the enamel was flawless, and the delicate pink flowers stood out beautifully against the turquoise background and gold accenting. Despite its feminine touch, the ring was stunning. "I'd be lucky to wear something so beautiful every day for the rest of my life as your partner."

Ezra radiated with joy as he took the ring back from me, only to slide it on my finger like we were getting married. "I knew you'd like it!"

"I love it." I was surprised to find it fit perfectly, almost like it had been made especially for me. It truly was a work of art in its own right. The ring looked right at home on my hand, complementing my numerous flower tattoos. "It's just as perfect as you promised."

"I made it, so of course it is." Etienne chuckled as he handed the *Starry Night* ring to me to inspect.

It was as perfect as the ten-dollar bill that had brought Ezra into my life in a twist of fate. I took his hand in mine and slid the ring onto his finger. The gesture was surprisingly intimate. "It's as perfect and wonderful as you."

Ezra's sunny smile brightened my entire world. He was downright giddy as he twisted the ring on his finger to see the full wrap of the artwork. "Etienne, they're everything I had hoped they'd be. We'll take them."

I reached into my pocket to pull out my wallet, but the Frenchman tutted at me with a shake of his head. "*Non*, there is no need. These are my wedding gift to you."

"Thank you, but that's too generous," I protested. "You're an incredible artist and deserve to be supported."

"You can pay me by giving Ezra the lifetime of happiness he deserves." Etienne gave me a charming smile. "That is worth more to me than any money."

"I'll do everything in my power to do that."

Ezra responded by giving me a hug that was so

strong it forced me back a few steps as I held him to steady myself. "I love you so much!"

Even though it had only been a short time since we had met, I had no problem returning the senti-ment. "And I love you just as much."

He looked up at me with a mischievous glint in his eyes. "Are you ready to get married for real?"

Chapter Twenty-Two

EZRA

"WHAT DO you mean get married for real?" Mauricio asked me.

I had originally planned on waiting, but damn it all to hell, I wanted him to be my husband today. "Were you serious when you said you'd marry me today? Because I'm ready to do it now."

Rather than answering, he posed a different question. "What about our family and friends? Don't you want them there to be a part of it?"

It was a fair point. "We can have a big fancy ceremony with everyone later once they're used to the idea of us being together. But I want to be your husband right now. I don't want to wait months for them to arbitrarily decide we've waited an appropriate length of time to commit to a marriage."

His green gaze softened with fondness. "Patience definitely isn't your strong suit."

"It really isn't." I took his hand in mine, rubbing my thumb over his ring. "What do you say? Will you marry me today?"

"Yes, I happily will get married to you today." He leaned down to give me a kiss that made me squeal with joy as I kissed him back like we weren't out in public with people watching.

We got a smattering of applause from some of the other people in the jewelry store, making me laugh when I pulled back. "Then I guess our next stop is City Hall."

Etienne chuckled. "You're as wild as ever, *mon frère*. Nothing can stand in your way once you make up your mind."

I bit my lower lip as I looked over at my closest friend. "Do you think I'm making a mistake?"

"Following your heart is never a mistake. Especially when it leads you to someone like him." Etienne tilted his head in Mauricio's direction. "As long as I'm allowed to be the best man at your proper wedding someday, I'm okay with your rash impulsiveness today."

His support overjoyed me. Leaning over the

counter, I tugged him down to kiss his cheek. "You've got yourself a deal."

He ruffled my hair with a grin before he pulled out two ring boxes. "Use these so you can actually exchange rings once you're having your ceremony. Now, go off with my blessing. Best wishes on your marriage, *mon frère*."

We gratefully accepted the boxes as we took off our rings to put them in and then exchange them later. I couldn't wait to wear our rings forever. They really were perfect for us.

After a few more words and another hug goodbye from Etienne, Mauricio and I set out for City Hall to get our marriage license and have a civil ceremony. Sure, it felt wrong and selfish to exclude everyone in the interest of expediting our wedding. However, I loved the idea of having something private just for us without the circus of our family and friends turning up and making it a chaotic celebration. Having it be just us had its own romantic appeal.

Everything went smoothly until we were informed there was a twenty-four-hour waiting period after the marriage license was finalized before we could have a ceremony. We also needed a witness, so hopefully, Etienne wouldn't mind coming with us to the court house tomorrow.

I continued fussing as we returned back to my apartment. "It's so stupid that there's a waiting period between getting your marriage license and actually being allowed to get married. How many people does that realistically stop from making a bad decision about who they're getting married to?"

"Probably not many, but it's fine." Mauricio wrapped me up in his strong arms as we stood in my living room. "What's a one-day delay when we have the rest of our lives to spend together?"

I sighed as I melted against him. "Yeah, you're right. But it's still annoying."

"Would using the time to book us a honeymoon make you feel better?"

I looked up at him with an excited noise. "Really? We can do that?"

"As long as you can get off work, I don't see why not. I'm a freelancer, so I make my own hours. If you don't mind me checking my email a couple of times while we're gone, I'm free to travel right now."

"I wouldn't mind at all, as long as I can do the same." It thrilled me that there was one less roadblock in our way. "Thankfully, I work whenever I want on whatever commissions I feel like, so it gives me a lot of freedom with my schedule. I don't have any immediate deadlines to worry about, so now is the perfect time."

He grinned. "How fortuitous. It's almost like fate decided now was the perfect time to bring us together."

"Right?" I laughed, but it brought up something that I realized needed to be discussed. Since I was marrying Mauricio, I owed him the truth about my past. "There really isn't a non-awkward way to say this, so I hope it doesn't change things between us. Not that I think it will with you, but it would with a lot of people, and—"

He led me over to my couch to take a seat. "Whatever it is, I'm sure it's fine."

Mauricio was right. I knew he wouldn't judge me the same way most people would. I took a deep breath and told him the truth that very few people knew about me.

Chapter Twenty-Three

MAURICIO

I WASN'T sure why Ezra looked so nervous, but I found out when he confessed something surprising.

"My mom died when I was a kid, and my dad passed away a couple of years ago. They left me with a sizable trust, so I don't actually need to work. I just do art for the sake of doing art."

Suddenly, his apartment with the nice view of the Brooklyn Bridge and his rich friend Etienne with the high-end jewelry store made a lot more sense. But my concern was the slight hint of fear I saw on Ezra's face. "I'm sorry about losing your parents. I can't even imagine how tough that was for you."

"It wasn't great," he said with a wan smile. "But

now, I have the freedom to do whatever I want. I usually don't tell people because once they smell money on me, they turn greedy. But I know you aren't one of those."

"You're still you, whether you have a dollar or a million in your bank account."

He sheepishly rubbed the back of his head. "Um, it's quite a bit more than that. My dad was a bigwig investment banker who came from old money. So we're pretty much set for life. We can go anywhere in the world for our honeymoon."

It was a generous offer, but I needed to be clear. "I don't want you to ever think I'm using you for your money. I'll contribute my fair share."

"All I need is cake and your love." He threw his arms around me as he buried his face against my neck. "Just tell me where you want to go, and I'll make it happen."

"I always imagined going somewhere tropical like an overwater bungalow, but wherever you want to go is fine with me. If you prefer snow instead of sand, I'm happy to go be a snow bunny with you."

He laughed at that, losing all trace of worry. "As cute as that sounds, I'd rather see more of your naked body out in the sun than all bundled up while we half freeze to death in some arctic tundra."

"You could always surprise me since that seems to be the thing you love the most." I grinned when he perked up at that. "I've enjoyed all your other surprises so far, so I'm sure whatever you arrange will be perfect."

He gave me a quick kiss before getting up and going over to the small desk where his laptop was. "You really are perfect for me. I've got a great idea. I promise you're going to love it. Let me see if we can do it. Do you have a valid passport?"

"Not on me, but I do at my apartment." I waited on the couch as he started working on his computer. "It won't take long to grab it when I go home to pack."

As he worked, I took out my phone and used the time to answer some emails and check social media. It really was the perfect time to take a vacation since I didn't have any pressing deadlines.

I lost track of time until I heard him proudly declare, "Done!" He came over and got in my lap again, so I wrapped my arms around him. "You're going to be *so* surprised. I can't wait!"

If it made him happy, I didn't care where we went. "You'll have to at least tell me what weather to pack for."

"To be on the safe side, pack for everything. I

can promise you it'll be the best honeymoon of a lifetime."

How could I ever say no to that?

Chapter Twenty-Four

MAURICIO TREATED me to yet another delicious dinner, making me even more excited to spend the rest of my life with a man who knew his way around a kitchen. I wanted to show him my appreciation, but I also knew I should show restraint.

It left me antsy as we did the dishes, causing him to laugh when he noticed. "What's gotten into you?"

"I'm torn."

"About what?" He dried his hands on a towel after we finished putting the last plate in the dishwasher.

"Because I *really* want to show you how much I appreciate you and your amazing culinary talents, but I also want to save it for the honeymoon to make it more special. I'm torn between doing what I should and what I want."

He grinned at my predicament. "Do I get a vote in the matter?"

"That's fair." I walked over to embrace him, resting my chin on his chest as I looked up at him. "What do you think we should do?"

"A compromise seems ideal here."

I could feel my dick starting to perk up at his words. "How do you mean?"

"We could settle for touching each other all over without penetration until we find release. Or I could use a dildo to bring you pleasure so you get relief without it actually being me inside you."

"No, if anything is going to be inside me tonight, it's going to be you." I tugged him down for a demanding kiss that he submitted to. "I refuse to be satisfied with silicone toys when I could have your dick spreading me open instead."

He chuckled, the low sound of it sending a shudder through me. "Is that your answer?"

My willpower was too weak in the face of my desire for the man who would officially be my husband tomorrow. "Let's start with touching first and see where that takes us."

Mauricio led me over to my bed, where we took

our time stripping each other of our clothes before falling into bed together. He pulled my body flush against his as we became a tangle of limbs while kissing and letting our hands roam over each other. Even the light petting drove me wild as I rutted against his thigh to find relief from how turned on I was from simple caresses.

I greedily let my hands travel over his body, delighting in every sharp inhale I caused as I ghosted over his sensitive spots. As I traced the map of his body with my fingertips, I memorized every inch of him and claimed it as mine.

When I tweaked his nipple, he tugged on my lower lip with his teeth. It made me jerk against him as my hips rocked against him. Everything felt good, but I was dying for relief. Taking matters into my own hand, I started pumping his dick in the hopes he'd get the hint.

Thankfully, he had no problems returning the favor. He reached between us and started stroking me with tantalizing slowness that no amount of desperately thrusting into his hand would speed up.

It pushed me to the point of desperation. "Please, I need more," I whimpered against his lips. When he didn't react, I pushed him onto his back and straddled over him. I rubbed my cock against his with a groan. "I need you, Mauricio. *Please!*"

He wrapped his hand around both of our dicks and began rubbing them against each other with the most exquisite friction. "I suppose this is still covered under the stipulation of touching only," he said, amusement lacing his tone.

I answered him with a hungry kiss as I devoured him with the fiery need driving my lust. My hips thrust harder against him as I picked up speed. He squeezed us together as he pumped us, which made me moan as I rocked against him in a ceaseless rhythm. It all felt so good, but it kept me on edge.

"Fuck, want you in me so bad," I whined as I wished he was deep inside me. "Want to feel you spilling out of me. *Mauricio!*"

Why had I been so foolish to suggest we stick to only touching?

Chapter Twenty-Five

MAURICIO

MY LUST WARRED with my sense of decency that wanted to obey Ezra's wishes that we stick to nonpenetrative forms of foreplay before the honeymoon. I owed it to him to remind him of his original intentions. "But you said you wanted to save that for the honeymoon."

"I was stupid." He keened with frustration. "Fuck, I need to come so bad! *Please!*"

His desperate pleas forced my body into reacting. I flipped us over to pin him on the bed. Reaching over to where we had abandoned the lube earlier, I dispensed some onto my fingers as I slid two of them inside his tight channel at the same time I went down on him.

Ezra's body jerked under me as he cried out, but I didn't let up. I sucked his dick with great pleasure while I pumped my fingers in and out of him. He desperately thrust his dick deeper into my mouth, and I opened wider to take more of him. It was why it came as such a surprise when his hands stopped me.

Before I could ask what was wrong, Ezra reversed our positions with a surprising show of dexterity and strength. He guided my arousal to penetrate him, but I had to protest. "You're not ready to—"

"Oh, I'm *more* than ready." He proved his point by riding me hard. I gripped his thighs tightly as I thrust up to meet his bounces, making him cry out as he tossed his head back with wild abandon. It was beautiful watching him derive so much pleasure from our bodies connecting. His exquisite ecstasy drove me to madness as he grew almost hoarse from crying out my name for all his neighbors to hear. But I was too lost in the experience to remind him that we might be disturbing people.

Instead, I raced toward my climax as we set a furious pace while I drilled him hard. He jerked off with increasingly desperate keens, his body moving nonstop with an increasingly frenzied need for more. Neither of us would last long at that pace, especially not after so much teasing.

He succumbed first, spilling his seed all over my stomach with a strangled shout of my name getting caught in his throat. I pulled him down on a forceful thrust as I came inside him in spurts until I was spent. I could feel my cum slowly seeping out of him as he shuddered on top of me with a whimper.

When he leaned forward to kiss me with a tenderness that was in stark contrast to the hard way he had been riding me, I slipped out of him, along with more of my release. It was obscene and filthy, but I couldn't get enough of it. I loved that he was covered in proof that he was mine. And after tomorrow, he'd be mine to love forever as my lawfully wedded husband.

I had never expected to get married or under such strange circumstances, but Ezra was already the best thing to ever happen to me. I couldn't wait to escape the city with him and start our honeymoon in whatever exotic location he had picked. It didn't matter where he picked, as long as we were together.

He collapsed against me in a boneless puddle with a satisfied groan. I wrapped my arms around him to hold him closer, in no rush to move. Getting clean could wait. All I needed in that moment was the feeling of closeness between us as I held him while recovering from our exertion.

Chapter Twenty-Six

EZRA

AFTER ENDURING the hassle of filling out more paperwork for the privilege to hurry up and wait, I fidgeted in the horseshoe-shaped atrium on the ugliest green couch I had ever seen.

Mauricio reached over and cupped his hand against the back of my neck to give it a reassuring squeeze. "Hang in there. Our number is coming up soon."

Etienne watched me with an amused smirk. "Are you okay, *mon frère*?"

"You know I suck at waiting." It was an epic understatement. I had a severe lack of patience when it came to that. Forcing myself to take a deep breath, I tried to draw on my fiancé's sense of calm.

"We've got nothing but time," Mauricio

reminded me. "There's no point in rushing a moment like this. It's worth waiting for."

"You're right." I leaned over and gave him a kiss. "Sorry."

His thumb brushed against the side of my throat, making me shiver. "There's nothing to be sorry about."

"But don't you think it's weird we're not actually at the courthouse? I thought all civil wedding ceremonies took place there." That's what the movies showed, anyway.

"I think it's nice they've set up these little makeshift chapels. It makes it feel a little more personal, don't you think?"

Before I could respond, our number was called. My heart rate picked up as the three of us entered the small room. The back wall was pink with a rainbow stripe painting. In front of it was a small wooden podium, where the officiant was waiting for us. There was a purple couch off to the right, where Etienne took a seat and pulled out his camera to memorialize our wedding ceremony.

As previously instructed, we put our wedding bands on the podium before I faced Mauricio as we joined hands. He was so handsome in his formal tuxedo that it took my breath away. I loved him for dressing up and not wearing a simple suit.

The officiant was an older gentleman in a nice suit who had a friendly smile. "Ready?" We both nodded. "Great, then let's begin. We are gathered here today to join Mauricio Damiano and Ezra van Housteen in marriage. You may exchange vows."

Mauricio went first. "Ezra, I promise to love, honor, and cherish you, through sickness and health, in poverty and wealth, and to always be true to you until death alone shall part us."

His words sent a thrilling rush through me that we were getting married for real. "Mauricio, I promise to love, cherish, and honor you in sickness and in health, in poverty and wealth, and to always be true to you until death do us part."

The officiant continued the ceremony. "Mauricio, do you take this man to be your lawfully wedded husband to live together in matrimony from this day forward, as long as you both shall live?"

"I do," he answered while smiling at me.

"Ezra, do you take this man to be your lawfully wedded husband to live together in matrimony from this day forward, as long as you both shall live?"

Joy overflowed in my heart. "I do."

"Wonderful." The officiant gestured at the wedding bands on the podium. "You may now exchange rings."

Mauricio picked up my band and took my hand. He looked deep into my eyes as he swore to me. "With this ring, I, Mauricio, take you, Ezra, to be no one other than yourself. Loving what I know of you, and trusting in what I'll learn to love, I will always respect and honor you with honesty and undying love, through all our years, in the face of anything that life may bring us." He slid the band onto my finger as I tried not to tear up from his beautiful words. It was the most romantic thing anyone had ever said to me. I was the luckiest man in the world to have someone so wonderful love me.

I had to take a steadying breath as I tried to get control of my emotions. It was a challenge when I was overwhelmed by how much I loved the man standing before me. "With this ring, I, Ezra, take you, Mauricio, to love with all my heart and everything that I am. This is only the start of the next chapter in our lives together, and I celebrate the love between us that continues to strengthen and grow with each day we spend together." My hand shook as I slid the band onto his finger, but I felt the rightness of what we were doing all the way in the depths of my soul.

The officiant gestured to us both. "By the power vested in me by the state of New York, I now pronounce you husband and husband. You may now kiss your spouse."

I savored the sweet kiss Mauricio gave me as Etienne cheered for us. It may not have been the huge grand wedding that I was supposed to desire, but I had everything I needed with my new husband. I thanked every lucky star that had brought us together. He really was the greatest wish come true. And now he was my husband to love for the rest of our lives together. I couldn't wait to see what the future would bring for us.

"You call that a kiss?" Etienne called out playfully.

"He's right," I said with a grin. "We can do better than that." I tugged Mauricio closer for a more passionate kiss, loving how it made him laugh as he hugged me closer.

When we parted for breath, the officiant smiled at us. "Congratulations to you both. I wish you a lifetime full of love and happiness together."

"Thank you," I said as I beamed at the man.

"We appreciate you being a part of our love story," Mauricio added.

The man tilted his head in acknowledgment. "It's my pleasure."

"Well, shall we go start our next adventure?" Mauricio asked as he held his hand out to me.

I took hold of his hand and gave it a squeeze as I grinned up at him. "Absolutely."

Epilogue

EZRA

BY THE TIME Mauricio had finished packing for our honeymoon, I was already slick and ready for him. I moaned as he pushed into me and started an easy rhythm that sent me soaring high. It felt amazing to have him filling the emptiness inside of me that had ached for so long until I met him.

I looped my arms over his neck as I held on tight while his body rocked me right. Knowing he was my loving husband making love to me made it feel even better than before. I hooked my ankles under his ass to give me leverage as I moved in sync with him, helping him push even deeper into me. It made my toes curl with delight as I called out to him.

In his amazing bed, it felt like the height of

decadence to be fucked in the most comfortable fluffy cloud in the sky. I luxuriated under his gentle attention as he worshipped me with his love that I couldn't get enough of. His hands traveling over any part of me they could touch heightened my enjoyment as he took care of me like no one else ever had.

It fortified my belief that marrying Mauricio had been the right decision to make. Maybe the world would think we had lost our minds to do it so soon after meeting, but I didn't care about that at all. How could I when it felt so amazing to be his?

"I can't believe you're mine to worship and adore for the rest of our lives," he murmured as he continued sending me to new heights with every thrust of his hips. "My beautiful husband."

His words sent a burst of pleasure through me. "I love you so much."

"Now, and for the rest of our lives." He brought my hand up to his lips to place a reverent kiss on my wedding band. "I really am the luckiest man alive."

"Yeah, you are," I teased him. I delighted in his laughter. It made me stop him to reverse our positions so I could start riding him with a little more urgency. I tossed my head back as I rocked with wild abandon and let him fill me up inside. "Yes! So good!"

He pushed up on my downward bounces, making me scramble to brace myself on his firm stomach. I got louder as we continued, losing myself in the incredible feeling of our bodies connecting as one. It felt like he completed me and made me whole for the first time in my life. I felt drunk on the ecstasy of being together.

When he reached out to jerk me off, I lost my rhythm as I thrust into his hand with a needy whimper. It took an effort to find the balance of moving between the two sources of pleasure. But once I did, I got rougher in my search for pleasure as he took care of all my needs.

"I'm so close," I whined low in my throat as I moved with desperation. I was right on the cusp of release, with my body feeling like a tight rubber band that was ready to snap.

"Then paint my skin with your cum. Claim me as yours," he ordered in a commanding voice that sent me over the edge.

I came hard with a wordless cry as I shot my load in spurts on his stomach. But I didn't stop moving since he hadn't come yet.

Mauricio pushed me to my limits when he

reached down and coated his index finger in my cum to bring up to his mouth. He put on a show of sucking it clean before he came inside me with a soft moan that made me shudder as I felt his release on the most intimate level.

I braced my hands on the bed and leaned forward, allowing him to slip out of me, along with some of his release. It made me feel like his in the best of ways. I kissed him passionately, loving when he tugged me closer to deepen the kiss.

Being married to my soul mate was the best feeling in the world.

Curious where Mauricio and Ezra go on their honeymoon? **Read "Dream Destination" next to find out!**

Want to dive into something longer with a similar vibe? **Check out Bet on Love to start the Sunnyside universe adventure.**

Bet on Love
——————————
AVAILABLE NOW

After Rhys wakes up married to his best man, he never expects to fall in love with his new husband. Will their surprise romance survive the wedding bells?

If you love friends to lovers, dual bi awakening, second chance, gay romances that are sweet and steamy, **read Bet on Love next**!

Acknowledgments

I hope you enjoyed Mauricio and Ezra's whirlwind romance! I know this book was a little different than my norm because of the bite-sized chapters, but I hope you still enjoyed this quirky love adventure.

Special thanks goes out to my wonderful team of beta readers of Amy Mitchell, Lindsay Porter, Tammy Jones, Lisa Klein, Kylie Anderson, Cilla May, Dylan Pope, Jennifer Sharon, Missy Kretschmer, Ashley Krystalf, Lauren, Becca, Emma Hultgren, Fiona Tsang, and Kathryn McCombe! I'm so lucky to have such amazing friends who have cheered me on through my ups and downs this past year.

I'm grateful to my ARC readers and anyone who helps spread the word about my books through recommendations.

I'm so blessed to work with Pam and Sandra. It's an incredible gift that they're always able to help to make my books as amazing as possible.

I can't wait to meet again in **Bet on Love**!

About the Author

Ariella Zoelle writes steamy, funny, feel-good romances where love is meant to be celebrated, not suffered through. If you're in the mood for low-angst stories packed with heat, humor, and heart, dive into her books and let the swooning begin.

But sometimes, she craves a little more drama (and some growly shifters). In her **Zarina Aston** books, she crafts romantasy worlds full of passion, magic, and just the right amount of angst leading to an epic love story and happy ending.

If you believe love should hurt a little first, her **A.F. Zoelle** books deliver high-angst contemporary romances brimming with heartbreak, longing, and all the delicious tension before the hard-fought happily ever.

Be sure to follow Ariella Zoelle on social media and never miss a new book!